P9-DNZ-710

DISCARDED

WAYNE PUBLIC LIBRARY

APR 1 2 2006

SAMANTHA SAVES THE WEDDING

SAMANTHA · 1904

BY VALERIE TRIPP

ILLUSTRATIONS DAN ANDREASEN

VIGNETTES SUSAN MCALILEY

THE AMERICAN GIRLS COLLECTION®

Published by Pleasant Company Publications
Previously published in *American Girl*® magazine
© Copyright 2000 by Pleasant Company

All rights reserved. No part of this book may be used or reproduced in
any manner whatsoever without written permission except in the case of
brief quotations embodied in critical articles and reviews.

For information, address: Book Editor, Pleasant Company Publications,
8400 Fairway Place, P.O. Box 620998, Middleton, WI 53562.

Printed in Singapore.
00 01 02 03 04 05 06 07 TWP 10 9 8 7 6 5 4 3 2 1

The American Girls Collection® and logo, American Girls Short Stories™,
and the American Girl logo are trademarks of Pleasant Company.

Edited by Nancy Holyoke and Michelle Jones
Designed by Laura Moberly and Kimberly Strother
Art Directed by Julie Mierkiewicz and Kimberly Strother

Library of Congress Cataloging-in-Publication Data

Tripp, Valerie, 1951-
Samantha saves the wedding / by Valerie Tripp ; illustrations,
Dan Andreasen ; vignettes, Susan McAliley.
p. cm. — (The American girls collection)
Summary: When Cornelia's veil is ruined on the day of her wedding
ceremony in 1904, nine-year-old Samantha comes to the rescue. Includes
information on wedding customs in the early 1900s and instructions for
making a bridesmaid bouquet.
ISBN 1-58485-035-3
[1. Weddings Fiction.] I. Andreasen, Dan, ill. II. Title. III. Series.
PZ7.T7363San 2000   [Fic]—dc21   99-38620 CIP

The
AMERICAN GIRLS
COLLECTION
™

OTHER AMERICAN GIRLS
SHORT STORIES:

FELICITY'S DANCING SHOES

AGAIN, JOSEFINA!

KIRSTEN AND THE NEW GIRL

ADDY'S LITTLE BROTHER

MOLLY AND THE MOVIE STAR

PICTURE CREDITS

The following individuals and organizations have generously given permission to reprint illustrations contained in "Looking Back": p. 32—Corbis/Bettmann; p. 33—Corbis/Hulton-Deutsch Collection; p. 34—Courtesy of Paula Moon; p. 36—Wedding Dress, ca. 1908-1918, Museum of the City of New York, gift of the Visconti/Nizza family; p. 37—Illustration by Jean-Paul Tibbles; p. 38—Corbis/Bettmann; p. 41—Corbis (wedding); p. 42—Photography by Jamie Young, Prop Styling by Jean doPico.

TABLE OF CONTENTS

SAMANTHA'S FAMILY

GRANDMARY
*Samantha's grandmother,
who wants her to be
a young lady.*

UNCLE GARD
*Samantha's favorite uncle,
who calls her Sam.*

SAMANTHA
*A nine-year-old orphan
who lives with her wealthy
grandmother.*

CORNELIA

*An old-fashioned beauty who
has newfangled ideas.*

AGNES & AGATHA

*Samantha's newest
friends, who are
Cornelia's sisters.*

ALICE

*Cornelia's youngest sister,
who is three years old.*

SAMANTHA SAVES THE WEDDING

R eady or not, here I come!" a voice called out. Samantha Parkington held her breath and tried not to move. She didn't want to give away her hiding place on the window seat behind the curtain.

Suddenly the curtain was thrust aside. A freckle-faced girl grinned at Samantha.

"Oh, Agnes! You found me too soon," said Samantha, laughing.

"I'm not Agnes," whispered the girl. "I'm Agatha. May I hide with you?"

"Sure," whispered Samantha. "Squinch in."

Agatha sat so close that her curls tickled Samantha's face and made her giggle. Soon both girls were giggling so much they didn't even hear Agnes enter the room.

The curtain was thrust aside again. "That was easy!" exclaimed Agnes. "You made more noise than the monkeys at the zoo."

Agnes looked exactly like Agatha. The twin girls were nine, just Samantha's age. Their older sister, Cornelia Pitt, was going to marry Samantha's Uncle Gard.

Samantha, Agnes, and Agatha were
going to be bridesmaids in the wedding.

Samantha and her grandmother had
been invited to stay at the Pitt family's
elegant town house in New York City for
the entire week before the wedding. They
had been with the Pitts for three days so
far, and Samantha thought it was the

most fun she had ever had.

Agnes kicked off her shoes and started jumping from bed to bed. "Come on!" she said. "Let's jump like monkeys."

"But Agnes," said Samantha. "You haven't found Alice yet." Alice was the twins' three-year-old sister.

"Oops! I forgot Alice," cried Agnes. "She always hides in the sewing room. Let's go."

All three girls rushed down the hall. Agnes and Agatha rushed everywhere. Uncle Gard said Agnes and Agatha were like woodpeckers: cheerful, redheaded, noisy, flighty, and into everything. The girls found Alice sitting on the floor of the sewing room. A blanket covered most of her, but her feet stuck out. The older girls were too kind to laugh at Alice. Agnes lifted the blanket. "Here you are, Alice," she said. "I found you last of all."

Alice beamed. "That means I won," she said. "Let's play again."

"No, come jump on the beds with us," said Samantha. "We'll pretend we're monkeys."

"That won't take much pretending," said a deep voice. The girls turned to see Uncle Gard and Cornelia in the doorway. "Are you having fun with these rowdies, Sam?" he asked.

"Oh, yes!" said Samantha.

Cornelia gave Samantha a quick kiss. "We are all delighted to have you here," she said. "Now I need you and the twins to come with me. I've something to show you."

"Our bridesmaid dresses?" asked Agnes.

Cornelia smiled and nodded.

"Hurray!" shouted the twins.

"I want one, too," wailed Alice.

Samantha felt sorry for her. But then Uncle Gard said, "You come with me, Alice. We'll practice dancing. You *are* going to dance with me on my wedding day, aren't you?"

"Come on!" cried Agatha. The three girls ran down the stairs to Cornelia's

room and flung open the
door. When they saw
the lovely, lacy pink
dresses lying on the bed,
they shrieked with delight.

Mrs. Pitt came into the room with
Grandmary. "Great Caesar's ghost,
girls!" she scolded. "Have a care for my
poor nerves!" Mrs. Pitt lowered herself
into a chair and held a handkerchief to
her forehead.

"Yes, ma'am," said the girls. They
couldn't wait to try on their new dresses
and were already halfway out of their
clothes.

Mrs. Pitt sighed and said to
Grandmary, "I think Agnes, Agatha, and

Samantha are too young to be bridesmaids, but Cornelia insisted upon it. I
do hope they'll behave properly during
the wedding."

Samantha was glad her face was
hidden as she pulled her bridesmaid
dress over her head. She was sure her
cheeks were pink from hurt pride.
How could Mrs. Pitt say such things?
Samantha would *never* embarrass
Cornelia—and especially not on her
wedding day.

"I'm sure they'll behave like proper
young ladies," replied Grandmary
calmly.

"Young, indeed!" Mrs. Pitt said.
"They are most exceptionally young."

"And they will be most exceptionally fine bridesmaids," said Cornelia. "I am sure."

Samantha poked her head out of her dress and flashed Cornelia a grateful smile.

When all the buttons were buttoned and sashes tied, Mrs. Pitt looked at the girls with a critical eye. "You look quite presentable," she said. "Take off the dresses now. Don't wrinkle them." And with that she swept out the door.

Grandmary paused long enough to say, "You young ladies look absolutely charming." And then she left, too.

"Cornelia," said Agatha when the girls had changed back into their usual clothes. "Please may we see your bridal gown?"

Cornelia opened the double doors of her wardrobe, and there it was—a creamy white dream of a dress decorated with tiny pearls from its high collar to its flowing train. "And here's the best part of all," said Cornelia. From behind the gown she carefully pulled a long white cascade of lace as light and fine as mist. "My veil."

"*Ooh,*" gasped the three girls.

Samantha sighed. "Oh, it's perfect."

Cornelia touched the veil gently. "Isn't it lovely?" she said. "I'll wear it only once, to mark the happiest day of my life."

It will be the happiest day of her life, thought Samantha. *I'll make sure it is.*

"Cornelia," said Agnes. "When I get married, may I wear this veil?"

"Yes, of course," said Cornelia. "And you, too, Agatha. And you, too, Samantha."

Samantha said softly, "Thank you.

But I . . . I already have a veil."

Everyone looked at Samantha with curiosity. "It was my mother's," she explained. "Grandmary said it belongs to me now. I've seen it only once or twice. It's in a box in the attic in Mount Bedford."

"How wonderful," said Cornelia. "Your mother has given you something precious to remember her by. I'm sure it's beautiful."

"Yes," said Samantha. "It's like your veil. It's long and white and puffy as a cloud."

Cornelia laughed. "My veil is as big as a cloud," she said. "In fact, I'd better find another place to keep it. I don't want it to be crushed." She grinned at the girls. "Well, my exceptional bridesmaids, run along now. I don't want you to use up all your good behavior before the wedding. Go find Alice and get into some mischief."

But the girls weren't interested in mischief. Instead, they decided to dress up as brides. Agatha found some old lace curtains in the sewing room. Each girl tied one around her waist to make a long, flowing skirt and draped another over her head to make a veil.

Suddenly Alice appeared. "I want a bride dress and veil, too!" she demanded. "Where's mine?"

"There are no more curtains," said

Agatha. "You can be the groom, Alice."

Alice frowned. "That's no fun!" she cried.

The girls had to admit she was right. So Samantha made a bride dress for Alice by pinning a pillowcase around her waist. For a veil, Alice wore one of Samantha's lace petticoats tied to her head with a ribbon.

The four girls practiced kneeling, sitting gracefully, and dancing. The older girls loved to swirl around and then sit down quickly to see their skirts and veils billow out around them. Alice was disappointed because her pillowcase and petticoat didn't swirl as well as the older girls' curtains did. So Samantha promised her that the next time they played dress-up she could have a better skirt and veil. That satisfied Alice, and the four brides played happily together all afternoon.

❧

The day of the wedding was wintry gray and cold, but inside the Pitts' house flowers bloomed on every table. Delicious smells floated out of the kitchen, the doorbell rang constantly, and excited voices filled the air. The four girls spent the morning upstairs smearing lemon paste on their faces to make their freckles fade. They tied their hair up in

rags to make it curly. Samantha didn't
actually have any freckles, and

Agnes, Agatha, and Alice
already had curly hair, but no
one wanted to miss out on
any of the fun.

About noon, the four girls wandered
downstairs. When Mrs. Pitt saw their
lemon-pasted faces, she cried, "Great
Caesar's ghost, girls! Don't be in the way.
The maid will come to help you dress at
five. Until then, you older girls keep an
eye on Alice." She fluttered her hands at
them and said, "Shoo!"

"Yes, ma'am," said the girls. They
scooted back upstairs.

Agatha asked restlessly, "What are

we supposed to do all afternoon?"

"Let's play hide-and-seek," said Samantha.

"No!" said Alice. "I want to play bride."

"We'll do that next," said Samantha. "Quick! Go hide now, Alice."

After a few minutes Samantha found Agnes and Agatha hiding under the beds. The three girls agreed that the lemon paste was making their faces itch, so they scrubbed it off. They pulled the rags out of their hair, too. They were just going to the sewing room to find Alice when Cornelia called to them.

"Come down, girls," she said. "Your bridesmaid bouquets are here!"

The older girls forgot all about Alice. They flew down the stairs. Grandmary, Mrs. Pitt, and Cornelia were waiting for them. Cornelia held three huge bouquets of lilacs in her arms.

"Here you are, ladies," she said. "Beautiful flowers for my beautiful bridesmaids."

The girls buried their faces in the bouquets to smell their lovely perfume.

Cornelia smiled and said, "Now take good care—" Suddenly the smile left her face and she gasped, "Alice!"

Everyone turned. Alice was coming downstairs draped in white from head to foot. Samantha stared, and then she gasped, too. Alice was wearing Cornelia's wedding veil! She had hacked it in two and used one part for a skirt and the other part for a veil. The lace hung in tatters. Cornelia's veil was ruined—completely, utterly, totally ruined.

"Great Caesar's ghost!" exclaimed Mrs. Pitt.

"No," said Alice cheerfully. "I'm not a ghost. I'm a bride! Now I have a swirly skirt, too!"

For a moment, no one moved or said a word. Then Grandmary groaned. Mrs. Pitt collapsed into a chair. Agnes and Agatha wailed, "Oh, Alice!" Poor Alice burst into tears. She could tell she had done something terribly wrong.

Alice was wearing Cornelia's wedding veil!

Cornelia was very pale.

"You older girls go to your room," said Grandmary quietly.

The three girls trudged upstairs and flopped onto their beds. *If only we'd known Cornelia put her veil in the sewing room this morning!* thought Samantha. *We could have warned Alice not to touch it. But now . . .* "We've got to do something," she said in a determined voice.

"What can we do?" asked Agatha. "The veil is ruined. We can't fix it."

"And it's one o'clock. The wedding's in five hours," said Agnes. "There's not enough time to get a new veil."

"Not a new veil," said Samantha slowly. "An old veil. I have a plan."

Samantha found Uncle Gard in the study. He listened to her carefully. When she finished, he looked at his pocket watch and shook his head. "It's awfully risky, Sam," he said.

"I'm not sure there's enough time to get to Mount Bedford and back, especially in this icy weather. We don't want Cornelia to come down the aisle with no veil only to find she has no groom, either."

Samantha was impatient. "Please, Uncle Gard. We've got to try."

Uncle Gard stood up. "You're right, Sam. We *do* have to try. Let's go!"

Samantha held her coat over her head as she rushed out of the house

and climbed into Uncle Gard's automobile. Sleet slashed at the windshield.
Soon Samantha was being bounced and
bumped as the automobile lurched along
the icy, rutted roads. Uncle Gard was driv-
ing fast. Even so, it seemed to Samantha
that the trip was taking ages. The sleet
so blurred the view that she couldn't see
familiar landmarks along the way.

When they finally pulled up to
Grandmary's house, Samantha hardly
waited for the automobile to stop before
she jumped out and ran up the slippery
steps. She hammered on the door with
both fists and called out to the maid,
"Elsa! It's me! Hurry! Open the door!"

Elsa opened the door and exclaimed,

"Miss Samantha! Sakes alive! Whatever's going on?"

But Samantha did not stop. She ran past Elsa and pounded up the stairs to the attic. She pushed hatboxes, shoe boxes, and dusty boxes of books out of her way until she found it—the box holding her mother's veil.

Samantha lifted the lid and looked at the delicate veil. It smelled faintly of rose petals, a smell that always made her think of her mother. The soft smell of roses was reassuring. It was as if her mother were giving her blessing to the idea of letting Cornelia wear her veil. Samantha closed the box and carried it down the stairs and out to the automobile.

She and Uncle Gard did not talk much on the trip back to the city. Samantha knew it must be getting late because the sky was darkening. *Please let us get back in time,* she thought. *Please!*

❧

At half past five, Samantha and Uncle Gard walked into the Pitts' town house—and into an uproar. "Where on earth have you two been?" cried Mrs. Pitt. She pushed her way toward them through a swarm of maids and musicians, waiters and florists.

Samantha left Uncle Gard to explain. She hurried up the stairs to Cornelia's room and tapped on the door.

"Why, Samantha!" said Cornelia when she opened the door. She was already wearing her wedding gown. "Everyone's been worried. Where have you been?"

"I have something for you, Cornelia," said Samantha. She set the box on the floor, knelt by it, and opened the lid. "It's my mother's veil," she said.

Cornelia sank to her knees next to Samantha. Slowly, she lifted the veil out of the box. "Oh," she said with a sigh. "It's so beautiful! I am honored to wear it." Cornelia had tears in her eyes, but she laughed as she said, "Oh, thank you, Samantha, thank you!"

Candles glowed in every window.
The music began. Exactly on cue, Agnes,
then Agatha, and then Samantha walked
down the flower-lined aisle to the graceful arch of greenery in front of the Pitts'
hearth. Mrs. Pitt, Alice, and Grandmary
smiled at the girls from the first row of
chairs.

Uncle Gard stood by the hearth next
to the minister. His tie looked as if he had
tied it in a hurry. His hair was still damp.
But he looked happy. His smile broadened
as the three girls walked toward him. He
winked at Samantha.

Everyone murmured in delight as
they watched Cornelia walking slowly

*Samantha and Agnes and Agatha stood shoulder to shoulder—
three most exceptionally happy bridesmaids.*

down the aisle on her father's arm. Through the fine lace of the veil, Cornelia smiled at Uncle Gard. Then she, too, winked at Samantha.

Samantha felt her heart fill with love. She and Agnes and Agatha stood shoulder to shoulder—three most exceptionally happy bridesmaids.

VALERIE TRIPP

At 9 *Now*

My husband and I were married on the front steps of the house I grew up in—the steps where my sisters and I played bride in dress-up clothes when we were children. Our wedding day was exceptionally happy because all our family and friends were there to help us celebrate.

Valerie Tripp has written twenty-nine books in The American Girls Collection, including five about Samantha.

A PEEK INTO
THE PAST

Weddings in 1904

When Samantha was growing up, weddings were as elaborate and as elegant as a couple could afford. Society weddings like Uncle Gard and Cornelia's were splendid affairs that were

A courting couple

filled with tradition and followed the rules of proper behavior.

Young ladies and gentlemen of

society met when they were formally introduced at dinner parties, dances, or balls. They might also meet when a young lady's mother invited gentlemen to *call on*, or visit, her daughter.

Once a couple had been introduced, they were permitted to *court*, or spend time together. They might sit in the young lady's parlor talking or playing games. Or they could go bicycling or roller-skating, on sleigh rides, or to amusement parks.

A gentleman handing a rose to his sweetheart

When a gentleman was ready to propose, he asked his young lady for her hand in marriage. If she accepted, he asked her parents for their approval. Once they agreed, he slipped a ring onto the third finger of her left hand. This

tradition followed the belief that a vein ran from that finger directly to the heart.

During the engagement, couples exchanged love tokens, such as flowers, locks of hair, or small portraits. They also sent each other love letters and even used their postage stamps to communicate. If the stamp was placed upside down on the left-hand corner of the envelope, it meant "I love you." If it was on the line with the recipient's name, it meant "Accept my love."

Once a young lady was engaged, she had to plan her wedding. The first thing she did was decide on a date. For many brides-to-be, the day, the month, even the hour of the wedding had important meaning. Each day of the week and month of the year had a rhyme that told its importance. June was one of the most popular months because it might mean an exciting honeymoon: "Marry when June roses grow,

Some young ladies kept their love letters in silk pockets.

over land and sea you'll go." Some people
believed that the best day of all to marry
was on the groom's birthday.

Many brides spent months planning
their weddings. They read ladies' magazines and newspaper accounts of
society weddings, such as Consuelo
Vanderbilt's wedding to the
Duke of Marlborough—the
most fashionable wedding
of the time.

The most important thing
a bride had to plan was her
trousseau (troo-SO), or outfit.
Turn-of-the-century brides
wore white silk or satin
wedding gowns with

Consuelo Vanderbilt and the Duke of Marlborough

graceful, sweeping trains. The dresses were often embroidered with delicate flowers, pearls, lace, and ribbons.

When they planned their trousseau, many brides followed the saying:

Something old,
Something new,
Something borrowed,
Something blue,
And a silver sixpence in her shoe.

In 1906, the newspapers wrote about White House bride Alice Roosevelt, the daughter of President Theodore Roosevelt.

She wore a cream satin dress with an 18-foot silver brocade train. Soon after the wedding, ladies' magazines reported that silver bridal trimmings were the newest fashion.

Alice Roosevelt

38

Brides often carried large bouquets. In the Victorian language of flowers, each flower a bride carried had a special meaning. Roses meant love, lilacs meant first love, lilies of the valley meant the couple would receive much happiness, and orange blossoms meant they would have many children. Bridesmaids carried *tussie-mussies*, or small bouquets of flowers. Many brides chose their sisters or

Bridal bouquet

their closest friends to be their bridesmaids. Some weddings had as many as eight or ten bridesmaids.

Before the wedding, the bride and her bridesmaids celebrated with a luncheon and a special "bridesmaids' cake." It had charms baked inside. Each bridesmaid could tell her future from the charm she found in her piece of cake. An anchor meant adventure, a horseshoe meant good luck, a heart meant true love, a flower meant blossoming love, a key meant a happy home, and a ring meant a blissful marriage.

A bride and groom got married at church or at the home of the bride's parents. Wherever the ceremony, the decorations were as elaborate as the couple's family could afford. Evergreens, potted palms, and huge sprays of flowers decorated the church. At home, rooms were decorated with hearts or bells made from flowers. Many couples said their vows under a flower-covered

A wedding under a trellis and bell

trellis with a good-luck symbol such as a bell or a dove hanging from the arch. After the ceremony, there might be food, entertainment, and dancing.

As the couple left for their honeymoon, the wedding party might throw slippers at their carriage. If a slipper landed on top of the carriage, the couple was promised good luck forever.

41

An
American
Girls
Pastime

MAKE A
TUSSIE-MUSSIE

Send a friend a message in flowers.

When Cornelia planned her wedding, she chose her flowers according to their meanings. Her bridesmaids—Samantha, Agnes, and Agatha—carried lilac tussie-mussies. In the Victorian language of flowers, lilacs meant first love. Cornelia chose them because Gard was her first love.

Look at the flowers and their meanings on the next two pages. Then make your friend a pretty tussie-mussie with a special meaning.

Pansy
Thoughtfulness

Blue Periwinkle
Friendship

Rosemary
Remembrance

Red Rose
Love

Blue Violet
Faithfulness

FLOWERS

Forget-Me-Not
True love

Primrose
Confidence

Magnolia
Love of nature

Honeysuckle
Generosity

Geranium
True friendship

Daisy
Beauty

YOU WILL NEED:

Scissors

Flowers

String

Lace doily or hankie

2 ribbons, each 1 foot long

1. Cut off the leaves at the bottom of each flower, leaving 2 inches of bare stem.

2. Place the flowers and leaves in a pretty arrangement.

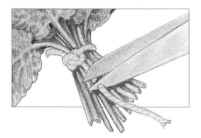

3. Tie the string in a double knot around the stems of the plants. Cut off the extra string.

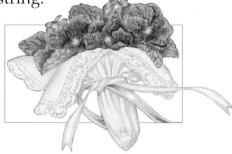

4. Wrap the lace doily or hankie around the stems. Then tie it in place with the ribbons.